This Little Tiger book belongs to:

_____

_____

_____

_____

For Shirin, Billy and Cameron
~L.J.

To Tony and his troublesome teeth!
~G.W.

LITTLE TIGER PRESS
An imprint of Magi Publications
1 The Coda Centre, 189 Munster Road, London SW6 6AW
www.littletigerpress.com
First published in Great Britain 2000
This edition published 2004
Text copyright © Linda Jennings 2000
Illustrations copyright © Gwyneth Williamson 2000
Linda Jennings and Gwyneth Williamson have asserted their
rights to be identified as the author and illustrator of this work
under the Copyright, Designs and Patents Act, 1988
A CIP catalogue record for this book is available from
the British Library
All rights reserved • ISBN 1 84506 065 2 • Printed in China
3 5 7 9 10 8 6 4 2

Titus's Troublesome Tooth

Linda Jennings and Gwyneth Williamson

LITTLE TIGER PRESS

London

Titus the Goat ate everything.
He ate carrots and cabbages.

He ate dandelions
and dockleaves.

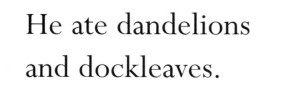

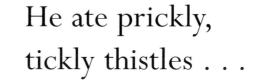

He ate prickly,
tickly thistles . . .

. . . and he even ate Farmer
Harry's pants and vests off
the washing line!

Titus absolutely
loved eating –
until one day . . .

. . . he woke up
with a terrible pain.

He didn't want
his breakfast . . .

and he didn't want to munch
and crunch the apples
in the orchard.

He wasn't even tempted to
nibble at Mrs Harry's nightdress.
Titus felt as miserable as . . .

. . . well, as miserable as a goat with toothache!
He was a very grouchy, grumbly goat indeed.

"That's a troublesome tooth," said Derry
the Donkey. "Open your mouth and I'll
pull it out with my big, strong teeth."

Titus shook from his
horns to the tip of his tail.
"Ooh-er, no thanks," he bleated.
He ran and ran and grouched
and grumbled . . .

. . . until he reached the farmyard.

"That's a troublesome tooth," said Sadie
the Hen. "Open your mouth and I'll peck
it out with my nice, sharp beak."

Titus quivered on all four hooves.

"Ooh-er, no thanks," he cried.

Titus ran and ran and grouched
and grumbled . . .

. . . until he reached the barn.
"That's a troublesome tooth,"
said Polly the Cat. "Open your
mouth and I'll scratch it
out with my long,
shiny claws."

Titus trembled from
his white beard to his
furry bottom.
"Ooh-er, no thanks,"
he shouted.

Titus ran and ran and
grouched and grumbled . . .

. . . until he
reached the meadow.
"That's a troublesome
tooth," said Basil the Bull. "Open your mouth and I'll
butt it out with my hard, curly horns."

All Titus's teeth chattered and
rattled – even the bad one!
"Ooh-er, no thanks," he sobbed.
Titus ran and ran and grouched
and grumbled . . .

. . . until he reached the duck pond.

"That's a troublesome tooth," said Daphne the
Duck. "Open your mouth and I'll tug it out with
some duckweed."

Titus shook so much that he nearly fell into the water.

"Ooh-er, no thanks," he yelled.

Titus ran and ran and grouched and grumbled . . .

. . . until he found himself right back in the farmyard again.

"Don't worry," said Sadie the Hen.
"Farmer Harry will get rid of
that troublesome tooth for you,
because he's called the Vet!"

"The Vet!"

shouted Titus.

He quivered and he shivered,
he trembled and he shook.
His teeth rattled and
chattered – even the bad one.
"No way do I want *the Vet!*"

Titus ran and ran . . .

and grouched . . .

and grumbled until . . .

...Titus bashed his head against the fence...

CRASH!

and the troublesome
tooth fell out at last!

Sink your teeth into a book from Little Tiger Press

Paul Bright   Ben Cort
Under the bed
Little Tiger Press

The Very Ugly Bug
Liz Pichon

Dilly Duckling
By Claire Freedman
Illustrated by Jane Chapman
Little Tiger Press

Here comes the Crocodile
Kathryn White
Illustrated by
Michael Terry

Don't be so nosy, Posy!
Nicola Grant
Illustrated by
Tim Warnes

Ready for Bed!
Jane Johnson
Illustrated by Gaby Hansen

For information regarding any of the above
titles or for our catalogue, please contact us:
Little Tiger Press, 1 The Coda Centre,
189 Munster Road, London SW6 6AW
Tel: 020 7385 6333 Fax: 020 7385 7333
Email: info@littletiger.co.uk
www.littletigerpress.com